Ants can hold a hundred times their own body weight.
Houseflies can walk upside down!
Ladybirds can be yellow, orange, brown, pink or even black!

For Fiz, who believed in
Betsy Buglove from the start – C.J.

For Robyn – L.F.

First published in 2021 by Scholastic Children's Books
Euston House, 24 Eversholt Street, London NW1 1DB
a division of Scholastic Ltd
www.scholastic.co.uk

London – New York – Toronto – Sydney – Aukland –
Mexico City – New Delhi – Hong Kong

ISBN PB: 978 07023 0566 5
ISBN HB: 978 07023 1037 9

Printed in China

10 9 8 7 6 5 4 3 2 1

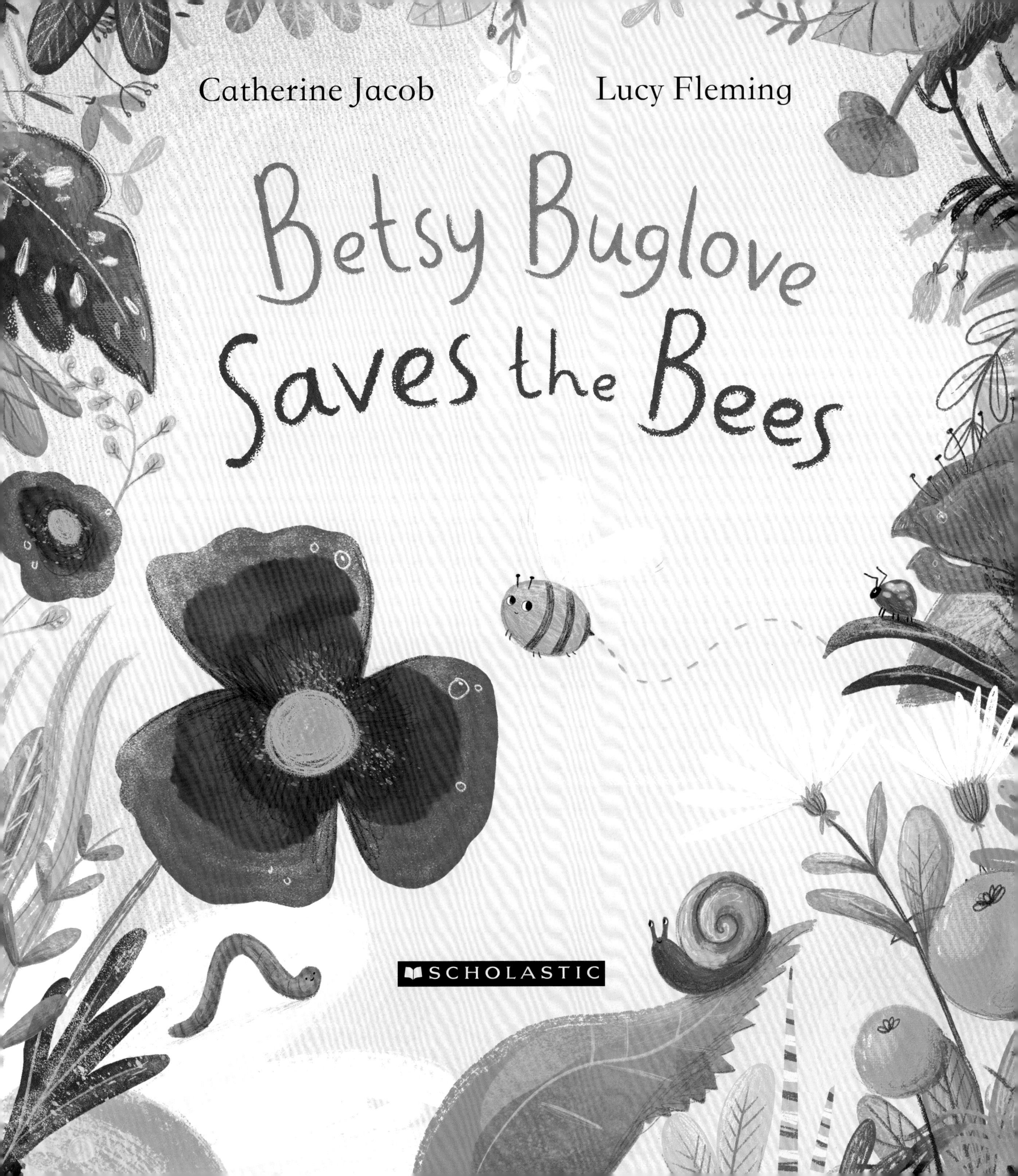
Catherine Jacob
Lucy Fleming
Betsy Buglove Saves the Bees
SCHOLASTIC

In a big, bustling town lived
a girl who **loved** bugs,

from earthworms

to ladybirds,

woodlice to slugs.

While spiders or ants might make some scream in fright,
to her, creepy-crawlies were such a delight!

Her name?

Betsy Buglove.
It suits her, it's true.

If you were an insect,
then she'd love you too!

If ever an insect fell into some trouble,
kind Betsy would be there to help, on the double.

A butterfly trapped in a web.

(Very sticky!)

A tangled-up centipede.

(That one was tricky!)

A slug who'd been caught
in the sun in a hurry.

With Betsy's sharp eyes,
no bug needed to worry.

Then, on Betsy's sixth birthday, her life was to change.

Her gran sent a gift,
with a note that seemed strange:

Dear Betsy, it read,
you remind me of me!
When I was a girl,
I loved bugs too, you see.
The present I've sent you,
is special. Unique!
For when you look through it,
You'll HEAR
INSECTS SPEAK!
Love Gran
x

So Betsy unwrapped it,
right there on the grass.

Inside it?

A magic magnifying glass!

She peered through the glass as some
ants marched on by.

"Climb over that rock, lads,"
she heard their chief cry.

A wasp whizzed along,
"Hey! Get out of my way!"

"Slow down!" called a snail,
"It's a beautiful day!"

"Where am I? I'm lost,"
buzzed a bumbling fly.

"This way," sang a spider,
a glint in her eye.

"I'm off to find veg,"
said a young caterpillar,
"My stomach is rumbling
and I need to fill 'er."

A honeybee buzzed around,
down in the clover.

"Hello!"

Betsy called as she
wandered on over.

The bee flew to Betsy.
Its buzzy voice cried:

"Oh, Betsy, please help us! We're all terrified!
It's Stan, from next door. He has just asked his dad
to pave over our garden – the whole lot!
It's so bad!"

"Your garden?" asked Betsy,
"The beds filled with flowers?"

"That's right!" buzzed the bee.
"They'll be gone in just hours!
Our flowers will die, and our grass and our trees.
It may not seem much, but it's home to us bees!

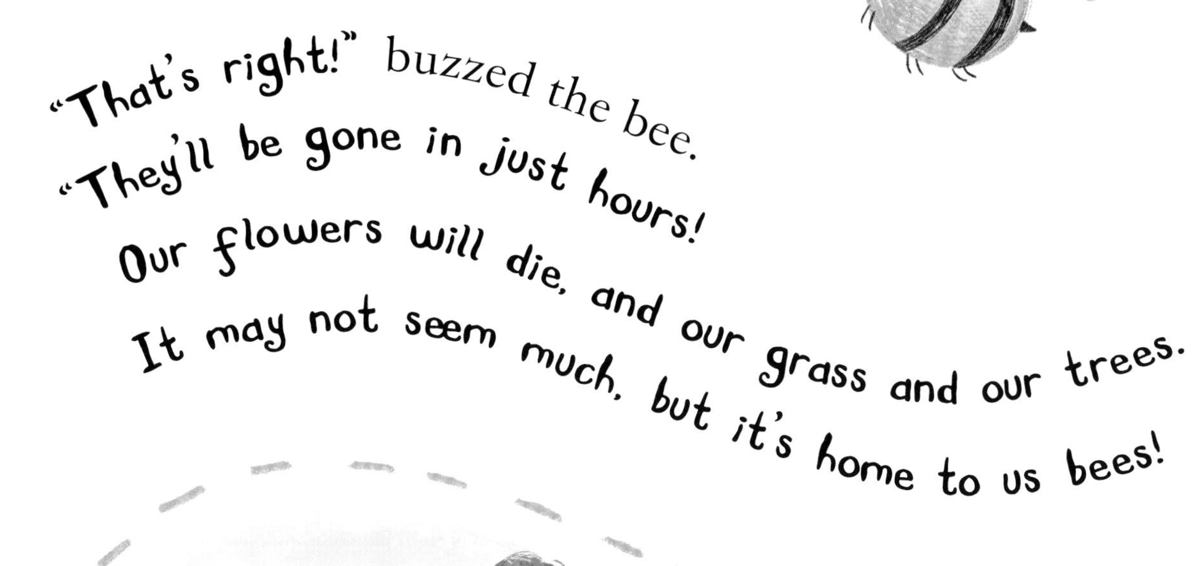

Stan's got a new bike and he wants the ground flat.
His dad's hired a digger. He'll dig. And that's that!"

"That boy **never** plays,
he's no fun," Betsy sighed.
"All those trees he could **climb**,
yet he's always inside."

"So what can we do?" buzzed the bee.
"We're so small,
and forgive me,
but you're just a child, after all."

"Don't stress!" Betsy said,
"It's not too late yet, is it?
Come on, bee. Let's go
and pay Stan a quick visit."

She knocked at Stan's door and she said: "Listen, please.
You can't pave your garden. It's home to the bees!"

"Are you kidding?" said Stan,
"Though I beg the bees' pardon.
Just tell them to go find another kid's garden!

I'll ride my bike here. Who are you to tell me what to do in my garden?

You can't! Go on, flee!"

As he slammed his front door, Betsy glowered at Stan.
"Come on, bees," she rallied, "let's hatch a new plan."

So the bees and the butterflies soon spread the word.
And soon, every bug in the garden had heard.

They scuttled and wriggled, they crept and they flew,
as Betsy described what she thought they should do.

"Let's go!" Betsy cried,
"For we don't have much time!"

The slugs and the snails started **oozing** out slime.

The bees made some honey, in fact they made **lots**,

and Betsy collected the **goo** in some pots.

The spiders got **spinning** . . . the silk worms got **sewing** . . .

And soon, an **enormous** cocoon started growing.

Then that afternoon, by a quarter past four,
their work was complete and she knocked on Stan's door.

The insects moved fast,
not a moment too soon.

Stan was trapped in their sticky cocoon.

"Now listen to me!" Betsy cried,

"Bees aren't mean.
They're hard-working heroes!
A farming machine!

It's time for you, Stanley, to go back to class.
Here, just take a look through my **magical** glass!"

"We bees spread the pollen from flower to flower.
Without us, the farmers would have little power

to grow things like strawberries, onions and peas.
Or blueberries, cherries, cucumbers . . . so, PLEASE

don't chop down your flowers. Their nectar feeds bees.
And as for our homes? Well, we live in your trees."

Stan stared in surprise. “Betsy, **please** set me free.
Here’s the reason I don’t like my garden: you see,

I am frightened of bugs!

They’re so **crawly** and **creepy**.

I don’t play outside as they make me feel **weepy**!”

So with Betsy's help (and her magical glass),
Stan soon had his nose buried down in the grass.

"I'll help you," Stan said,
"to let everyone know,
that it's really important
to let gardens grow."

So they soon spread the word,
and the flowers grew tall.

See, you CAN make a difference,
although you're quite small!

Stick insects can change colour.

Caterpillars have an enormous appetite: they're ALWAYS hungry.

Dung beetles survive by eating other animals' poop!

Earthworms breathe through
their skin and have no bones.
Woodlice can have up
to two hundred children!
Spiders have eight legs.
Praying mantises have
five beady eyes.